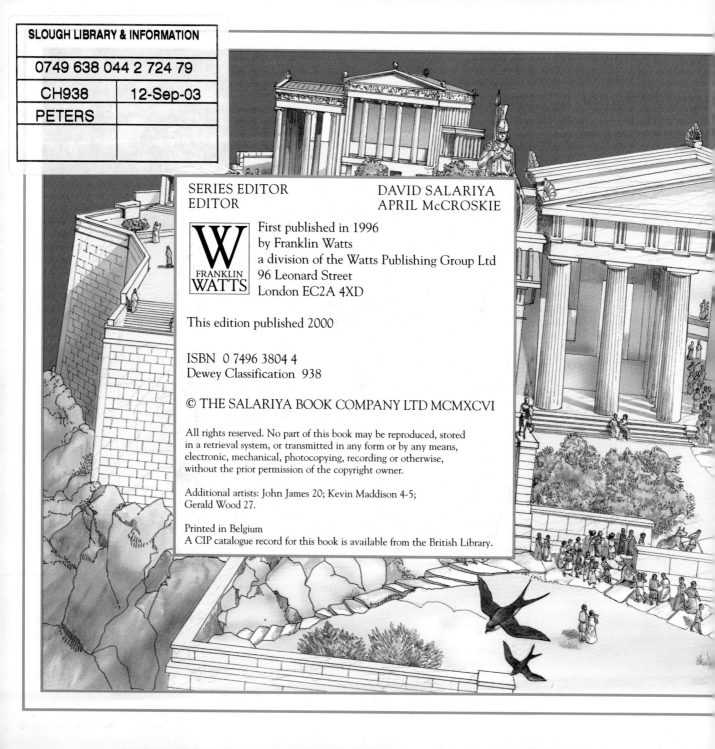

SERIES EDITOR   DAVID SALARIYA
EDITOR   APRIL McCROSKIE

W
FRANKLIN
WATTS

First published in 1996
by Franklin Watts
a division of the Watts Publishing Group Ltd
96 Leonard Street
London EC2A 4XD

This edition published 2000

ISBN 0 7496 3804 4
Dewey Classification 938

Additional artists: John James 20; Kevin Maddison 4-5;
Gerald Wood 27.

Printed in Belgium
A CIP catalogue record for this book is available from the British Library.

ancient
greeks

Written by
DAISY KERR

Illustrated by
MARK BERGIN

Series Created & Designed by
DAVID SALARIYA

FRANKLIN WATTS
LONDON•SYDNEY

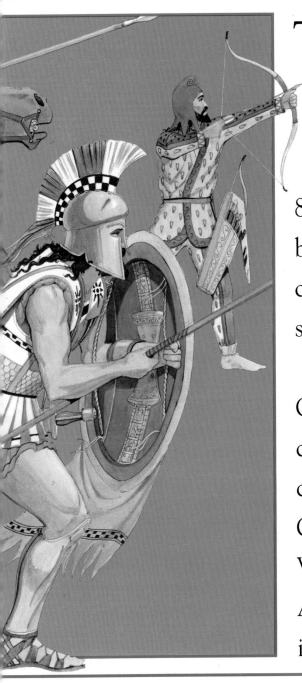

The ancient Greeks

lived over 2,500 years ago. Greek civilisation flourished from around 800-350 BC. Greek armies were brave and strong. Scholars were clever, craftworkers and artists were skilful, and merchants were rich.

Philip of Macedon conquered Greek lands in 338 BC, but Greek civilisation did not disappear completely. We still admire many Greek buildings and works of art. We still use some Greek words. And we still rely on many Greek inventions and discoveries today.

The Greek

people's homeland was present-day Greece. But the 'Greek world' stretched all around the Mediterranean Sea, from southern Europe to the north of Africa. Many Greek people lived in Cyprus and Turkey, and on islands off the Greek and Turkish coasts. Merchants sailed between these settlements. The Greeks built new towns in southern Italy and on the shores of the Black Sea.

MACEDON

Athens

GREECE

Sparta

MEDITERRANEAN SEA

CRETE

Area in red shows the Greek world.

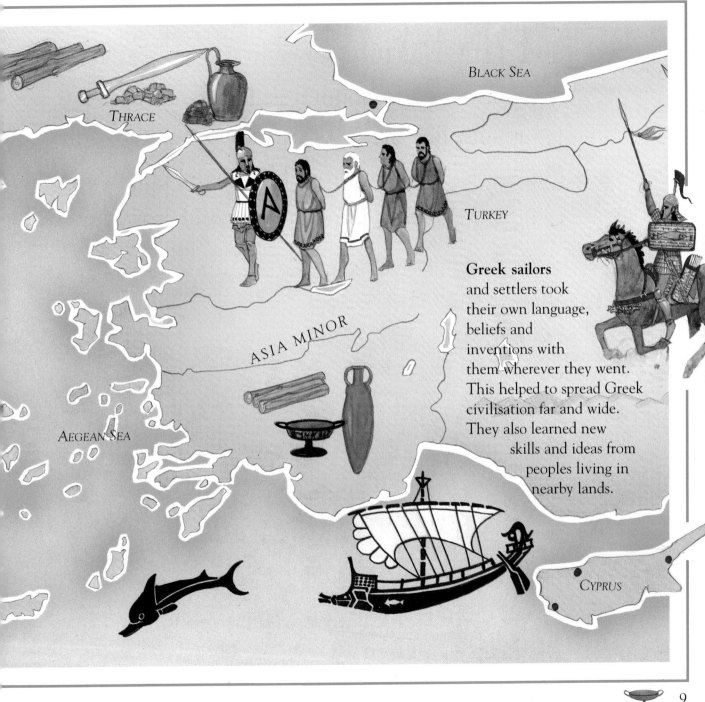

BLACK SEA

THRACE

TURKEY

ASIA MINOR

AEGEAN SEA

Greek sailors and settlers took their own language, beliefs and inventions with them wherever they went. This helped to spread Greek civilisation far and wide. They also learned new skills and ideas from peoples living in nearby lands.

CYPRUS

At harvest time, the whole family worked hard to collect ripe olives and press them to make oil.

The land of ancient Greece was very beautiful, with mountains, forests, cliffs and streams. But the soil was thin and stony. Only a few crops like olives, grapes and grain would grow there.

Olive trees

Picking olives

Olive oil

10

And only a few goats and tough mountain sheep could survive. The climate was harsh. Summers were very hot and sunny, but winters could be bitterly cold.

Greek farmhouses were made of rough stone, with roofs of clay tiles. Windows had strong wooden shutters to keep out robbers.

Courtyard

Farmhouse

Mountain sheep

Rough mountain road

11

Coins from Greek city-states. Each city's coin had a different design.

Slaves captured in wars were bought and sold in the agora (market-place).

Athenian citizens could go to the assembly to make speeches and pass new laws. Citizens could be members of a jury in the lawcourts, and help run the army.

Huge ivory statue of the goddess Athene. She protected the city of Athens.

The Greek world was divided up into many city-states. Each had a town, or a city, plus farm land all around. Athens was the biggest and most powerful city-state. It had a rich empire in foreign lands.

Ostraka

The Parthenon (built 447-438 BC) was a temple dedicated to the goddess Athene.

Citizens voted by casting clay ballots or ostraka into a big clay jar.

Ballot

Citizen soldiers kept guard outside the city gates and the city walls.

Pericles (top) was the most famous ruler of Athens. He lived around 500-429 BC. Socrates (bottom) was a famous Greek philosopher. He lived 470-399 BC. He taught his students to think and ask questions about life.

Early city-states were ruled by kings. Around 600 BC, they were replaced by powerful, rich men. After about 500 BC, many city-states became democracies. All adult males had the right to take part in government.

Silver coin made in Athens, decorated with an olive branch and Athene's owl.

Many non-Greek peoples also lived in Greek cities. Foreigners, women and children did not have citizens' rights.

Farmers brought fruit, oil, and grain into the city on mules. In wartime, enemy armies surrounded the city and cut off food supplies.

In 482 BC, the Athenians found silver close to the city. They sent criminals and slaves to dig deep mines. Conditions in the mines were terrible, but the city of Athens grew wealthy.

Athens had temples, theatres, sports halls, schools, government offices, shops and taverns.

In summertime, Greek cities were full of flies, because there were no sewers.

Houses in Greek cities were packed tightly together. Poor citizens lived in simple, single-storey homes.

In 450 BC, about 250,000 people lived in the city of Athens.

In early Greek times, most people lived and worked in the countryside. But after around 700 BC, they started to move to the cities. They found they could make a better living there, as shopkeepers, butchers, bakers, entertainers, and craftworkers of all kinds.

Wealthier citizens lived in well-planned homes, with rooms for preparing and cooking food, and entertaining guests.

The family said prayers at the altar every day.

Greek homes were often built around a courtyard, which let in sunlight and fresh air. They were protected from the dirt and bustle of city streets by strong gates and thick walls.

Bedroom

Upstairs, there were private rooms where women and their slaves worked and relaxed, away from male company.

Courtyard

Stool

Couch

Table

Meals were cooked over an open fire on a hearth made of large stones. Food was stored in large, rat-proof clay jars, called amphorae.

Craftsmen worked at home. Visitors came to their work-rooms to admire and buy craft goods.

Cities were busy, noisy, crowded and often very smelly. Overcrowding led to quarrels, riots, food shortages and disease.

Potters made jugs, bowls, vases and cups from clay, which was fired and then painted with beautiful designs.

Leather-workers made sandals, soldiers' boots and workers' aprons from ox-hide and goat skin.

Sculptors carved statues, tombstones and fancy columns for temples out of fine white marble stone.

There were many

well-trained craftworkers living in Greek cities – weavers, potters, painters, sculptors, goldsmiths and leather-workers. Some made solid, hard-wearing goods, like shoes and cooking pots, for ordinary people to use. Others produced beautiful masterpieces that only rich people could afford.

The simplest craft goods were home-made, by poor women. They spun thread and wove cloth to make rough cloaks, rugs and blankets to keep their families warm.

Kiln

Pottery was fired in a red-hot kiln. When it cooled, it was painted with pictures of gods, heroes or scenes from everyday life.

Upright loom

Greek men and women wore loose, simple and elegant clothes.

Engraved gemstone

Greek jewellers liked to engrave (carve) amazingly detailed pictures onto precious gemstones.

Women spun fine thread from the wool of sheep, then wove it into cloth on tall upright looms.

Necklace

Chiton

Peplos

Bracelet

Himation

The best stone-carvers and sculptors moved from city to city. They worked on temples, palaces and other fine buildings.

Greek goldsmiths created fabulous jewellery like this gold bracelet, decorated with animal heads, and this necklace of silver beads.

Women wore a floor-length tunic, called a peplos. Men wore a knee-length tunic called a chiton and a cloak called a himation.

Sandals and boots, suitable for Greece's hot, dry weather.

Athens

Macedon

Syracuse

Syracuse
(reverse of coin)

Corinth

Aegina

Coins were invented in Lydia (in present-day Turkey) around 690 BC. They were soon used all over Greece. Each city made its own out of silver or gold.

Traders weighed coins before accepting them to make sure they were real.

Buyers and sellers haggled over prices. Everyone wanted to find a bargain.

Farmers brought eggs and chickens to sell. There was no room in the city to grow food.

The market-place was the social centre of each Greek city. Citizens went there every day to buy food. They also went to the market to meet their friends to discuss local politics and the latest news.

In big towns, people could buy take-away foods from market stalls.

Men or slaves usually did all the shopping. Servants and slaves carried water from street fountains. 'Respectable' women stayed at home.

Fishermen carried fresh fish and seafood from the harbour to the market.

Few Greek people could afford to eat these favourite foods every day:
1. fish 2. squid
3. shellfish 4. fresh herbs 5. olives
6. figs 7. bread
8. chicken
9. cheese 10. ham

City-states grew rich by taxing trade. So they encouraged trade by building new markets, with rooms nearby where bankers and money-changers could work.

Greek men liked extravagant dinner parties. They ate rich food, drank wine mixed with water, listened to music and talked.

Wealthy families kept slaves as cooks, or hired them to prepare special meals. In ordinary families, the cooking was done by women.

Rich Greek people could afford beautifully-decorated cups and plates.

This cup, decorated with a ram's head, was for drinking water and wine.

Greek families ate foods like bread, beans, olives, grapes and figs. In summer, everyone ate fresh vegetables and herbs. In winter, they ate foods harvested in autumn and carefully stored, like apples, chestnuts, lentils and smelly goats' cheese.

Favourite entertainments were plays, music and dancing. Plays were staged in open-air theatres and performed by actors in masks and elaborate costumes. A performance might last all day. Many plays were written to criticise the government.

Theatres were built with sloping rows of seats in a half-circle shape.

Poor people were given money by the citizens to pay for cheap seats.

The largest Greek theatre, at Epidaurus, could seat around 14,000 people.

Greek actors were well trained. They had stamina and a good memory. Plays included dancing, singing and mime.

Actors wore comic (happy) or tragic (sad) masks, depending on the part they were playing.

Greek boys and girls were educated differently. Rich boys went to school, where they learned reading, writing, dancing, music and maths. Older boys might also study science, philosophy or law. Exercise was important, too. Boys from ordinary families were trained by their fathers in farming, trading or craft skills. All Greek girls were educated at home. Rich girls learned how to manage a household and give orders to slaves. Ordinary girls learned cooking, cleaning, weaving and child care.

The Greeks invented an alphabet – a way of writing using symbols for different sounds. We still use these letters in a modern form.

A	B	Γ	Δ	E	Z	H	Θ	I	K	Λ	M	N	Ξ
A	B	C	D	E	Z	E	Th	I	K	L	M	N	X
O	Π	P	Σ	T	Y	Φ	X	Ψ	Ω				
O	P	R	S	T	U	Ph	Kh	Ps	O				
				F	Ch								

Sappho, a poetess, lived in the 6th century BC. She was famous for her love poems.

This fragment of Sappho's poetry has survived.

Dancers

Lyre

Girls were trained to dance. Dancing was good exercise and formed an important part of many festivals.

Popular instruments included lyres, flutes, pan pipes, tambourines and the kithara – an early form of the guitar.

Greek men and women danced to the music of many different instruments.

The Acropolis was an ancient fortress built on a high rock in the centre of Athens. The Athenians built many fine temples there, to honour their gods and goddesses.

Priestesses, called oracles, claimed to be able to see into the future. They had visions after being drugged by poisonous smoke from burning laurel leaves. The most famous oracle was at Delphi.

Oracle

The Acropolis (high fortress) of Athens

The statue of Athene was about 17 metres high

Grand gateway

Ancient Greeks believed in

many different gods and goddesses. Some watched over cities and some controlled the crops. Some brought love and wealth, and others caused war, disease and death.

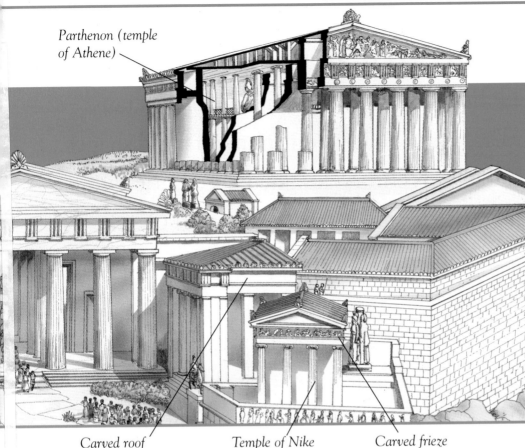

Parthenon (temple of Athene)

Carved roof

Temple of Nike (goddess of victory)

Carved frieze

Temples were built as houses for goddesses and gods. Temples were built of the finest stone and decorated with paintings, carvings and statues.

Zeus was king of the gods. He ruled the heavens and the earth.

Hera

Artemis

Apollo

The Greeks built magnificent temples for their gods and goddesses, and made offerings to them. They hoped the gods would help them in return.

Hera was queen of heaven and looked after women and children. Apollo was god of the sun. He played the lyre and inspired musicians. His twin sister, Artemis, was the goddess of hunting.

Pythagoras (572-497 BC), was a famous Greek mathematician. He started up a community of scholars, in southern Italy, to study maths and religion.

Greek astronomers studied the moon and the stars carefully. They named many groups of stars.

Greek geographers invented methods to calculate the distance around the world.

The ancient Greeks were skilled scientists. Greek mathematicians discovered rules about numbers and shapes. Greek inventors designed automatic doors and the first slot machines. And Greek geographers were the first to suggest that the world was round.

Greek medicine was a mixture of science and religion. Greek doctors believed that the gods helped healing. But they also discovered that our surroundings, our food and our state of mind all affect our health.

Archimedes' machine

Archimedes (287-212 BC), designed a machine to make water flow uphill. The design was used for almost 2,000 years.

Greek 'klepsydra' (water-clock)

Asclepius was the god of healing. His priests worked as doctors in temples.

Greek doctors were trained to make scientific examinations of their patients. This helped them understand and cure diseases.

Some patients chose faith-healing. They stayed overnight in temples. They hoped to be cured by a 'visit' from the god in a vision or a dream.

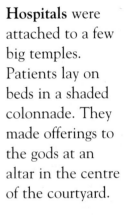

Hospitals were attached to a few big temples. Patients lay on beds in a shaded colonnade. They made offerings to the gods at an altar in the centre of the courtyard.

Patients who had been cured at a temple left offerings in the shape of the part of their body that had been healed.

Blood-letting

The Greeks believed that our bodies contain balanced amounts of four liquids. If this was disturbed, blood-letting (removing blood) put the balance right again.

Greek medical instruments – hooks, spatulas, probes and tongs, plus a pestle and mortar, used to grind herbs to make medicines.

Temples were designed with rows of columns supporting a massive roof. They were decorated with many fine carvings.

This frieze shows a battle between a man and a monster called a satyr.

Religious festivals played an important part in many Greek cities. They were held to honour all the different gods or goddesses. Sometimes festivals were held in memory of ancient local heroes, as well. Nobody worked on festival days. Instead, they said prayers at the temples, or danced in processions through the streets, playing music. People brought offerings, such as animals wearing beautiful flower garlands, to give to the gods and goddesses.

A beautiful frieze, carved in stone, was fixed around the top of the Parthenon building, about 12 metres above the ground. It shows a festival procession walking from the centre of the city of Athens to the altar of the goddess Athene, which stood in front of the Parthenon.

Olympia was an ancient holy site. Games were first held there in 776 BC, in honour of the god Zeus.

Arena for sports practice

Covered walkway, where athletes could walk and talk

Temple of Hera, one of the oldest buildings on site

Guest-house and sports practice ground

Many splendid buildings were built for visitors to stay in during the Olympic Games.

Athlete with helmet and shield

Sport was important to the Greeks. It was fun and good training for war too. Soldiers built up their strength by running in armour, throwing spears, wrestling and boxing. These sports were all useful when it came to fighting real enemies.

Treasury containing the riches of small cities protected by Olympia

Temple of Zeus, containing a massive gold and ivory statue

The stadium was almost 200 metres long and 30 metres wide. The race track was covered with white sand and the starting line was made of stone. Referees kept order with big sticks.

Female athlete

The Olympic Games were held for five days, every four years. Victorious sportsmen won fame and fortune. They were given a crown of leaves and ribbons, and prizes of olive oil, fine fabrics and pottery. Poems were written to praise them.

A separate sports festival, to honour the goddess Hera, was organised for women.

Coins showing riding; winner's crown of leaves; chariot racing.

Soldiers fighting in a phalanx formation

Greek soldiers fought with sharp iron swords, long, bronze-tipped spears and wooden shields. Weapons, helmets and armour were passed on proudly from father to son.

Greek city-states were often at war. They fought against one another, and they also fought together as friends against enemies from abroad. All men over 18 were expected to join the army. In Athens, young men had to spend two years training.

Greek soldiers fought mostly on foot. In battle, they advanced side by side in a 'phalanx' formation. This presented a wall of shields to the enemy. The soldiers of one phalanx threw their spears at another, hoping to make the enemy soldiers run away.

Some city-states had professional soldiers, recruited from nearby lands. They fought with sling-shots (strips of fabric for hurling stones) or with bows and arrows.

Each baby was examined by Spartan elders. If it was weak or sickly, it would not be allowed to live. Spartan women had to train hard and keep fit so they would have healthy babies.

Sparta was a city-state in southern Greece. It was not a democracy like Athens. Instead, it was ruled by two kings, a council of elders and an assembly. Only a few Spartan citizens were free. The rest were called helots and were treated like slaves.

Spartan boys were taken away to be trained and educated by the state.

Spartan soldiers stood guard over the helots working in the field in case they ran away.

Spartan wedding. Husbands spent most of their time away in the army.

Spartan citizens did not trade. Only non-citizens could work as merchants.

Helots were guarded, in case they tried to riot or run away. The helots hated the citizens, the elders and the kings. Spartan citizens lived simply, so they would always be ready for war. Rich foods, warm clothes and comfortable homes were forbidden.

Spartan women athletes trained hard.

Spartan women were trained to take part in games, so they would be fit and strong. Other Greeks were shocked by their short tunics.

Many important wars

were fought at sea. In a sea battle, enemy
warships tried to ram and sink one another.

Oars

Paddle

Stern

The biggest
Greek warships
were called
triremes. They
were rowed by 170
people, who kept
time to the music
of a flute. Triremes
were steered by
two huge paddles
at the stern.

The Persians (from
present-day Iran)
were the Greeks' most
powerful enemy. Persian
soldiers and sailors
invaded Greece in 490 BC
and again in 480 BC.

In 480 BC, the
Athenian navy, led by
General Themistocles,
destroyed Persian ships
at the battle of Salamis.
This battle defeated the
Persian invasion.

Battle
commander

Rows of
shields

Painted eye, to scare
away bad luck

Deck

Flute player helped
rowers keep time

If an attacking ship failed to sink its enemy, it sailed as
close as possible to it, so that the decks were side by side.
Then soldiers would leap on board and slaughter the
passengers and crew. Invading armies relied on sea
transport for carrying soldiers, weapons and food.

USEFUL WORDS

Agora Market-place.

Amphora Storage jar made of clay.

Astronomers People who study the sun, moon and stars.

Ballot Clay token used to vote.

Chiton Knee-length tunic.

Colonnade Covered walkway; a roof supported on columns.

Democracy A government where the people rule.

Empire Lands ruled by another, stronger country.

Engrave To carve a design on a hard, smooth surface.

Frieze Carved border fixed to a wall.

Helots Non-citizens who lived in Sparta. They were treated like slaves.

Himation Long cloak usually made of wool.

Oracle Priestess who claimed to be able to see into the future.

Ostraka Fragment of pottery on which Athenian citizens wrote the names of people they wanted to

ban from their city.

Peplos Long tunic, worn by women.

Pestle and mortar Heavy bowl and stick used to crush and grind herbs to make medicines.

Phalanx Row of foot-soldiers standing with their shields.

Philosophy The study of ideas.

Symposium Dinner party, for men only.

Trireme A fast Greek warship with three rows of oars.

INDEX